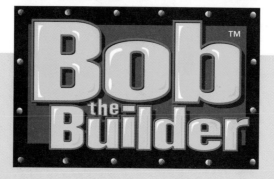

Bob's A to Z Word Book

adapted by
Kate Telfeyan

based on a book by
Rebecca Gerlings

designed by
Aviva Presby

SIMON SPOTLIGHT
New York   London   Toronto   Sydney

Based upon the television series *Bob the Builder*™ created by HIT Entertainment PLC
and Keith Chapman, as seen on Nick Jr.® Photos by HOT Animation.

SIMON SPOTLIGHT
An imprint of Simon & Schuster Children's Publishing Division
1230 Avenue of the Americas, New York, New York 10020

Manufactured in the United States of America

First Edition
2 4 6 8 10 9 7 5 3 1

ISBN 0-689-86503-1

A is for

Airplane

Armchair

Apples

B is for

Bricks

Brush

Bucket

Bob the **B**usy **B**uilder

C is for

Camera

Cone

Candle

Cake

D

is for

Doghouse

Ducks

Dizzy

E is for

Earrings

Envelopes

Eggs

F

is for

Finn **F**lipping . . .

out of his **F**ishtank

I is for

Igloo

Ice skating

Ice cream

J is for

Jog

Jump

Jug

K

Wendy likes to bake
in the **K**itchen

Dizzy likes to **K**ick
the soccer ball

L is for

Lofty **L**ifting up **L**ogs

M

is for

Muck who loves

being **M**uddy

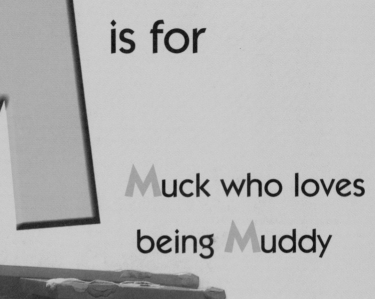

N

is for

Nest

Newspapers

O is for

Owl

Otters

Onions

Parrot eating **P**izza

P is for

Pilchard

Porcupines

Q

The ducks say
"**Q**uack,
Quack!"

R

is for

Roley

Raincoat

Rabbits

S

S is for

Spud
acting **S**illy

Scruffty

Scoop **S**hoveling
Snow

T is for

Travis **T**owing

his **T**railer

Turtle

U is for **U**mbrella

V is for **V**egetables

W

is for

Wendy
painting With
Watercolors

Can we fi**x** it?

X

Y

Yes,
we can!

Z

zzZZZZZZZZZZZ**z**